Marx Hardy Machiavelli Chesterton Cooper Emerson Joyce Austen
Abbott Defoe Melville Montaigne Haggard Hugo Grimm Eliot
Stoker Carroll Christie Molière
Wilde Maupassant Byron Schiller
Garnett Einstein Fitzgerald Engels Hawthorne Smith Kafka
Goethe Hawthorne Dostoyevsky Hall
Cotton Kipling Doyle Willis
Baum Henry Nietzsche
Leslie Dumas Flaubert Turgenev Balzac
Stockton Vatsyayana Crane
Burroughs Verne
Curtis Tocqueville Whitman Gogol Vinci
Homer Widger Tolstoy Busch
Darwin Thoreau Twain Plato Scott Harte
Potter Freud Zola Lawrence Dickens Burton Hesse
Kant Jowett Stevenson
Andersen Cervantes
London Descartes Voltaire
Poe Aristotle Wells Cooke
Hale James Hastings
Bunner Shakespeare Irving
Richter Chambers
Doré da Shaw Benedict Alcott
Chekhov Pushkin
Dante Wodehouse Newton
Swift

 tredition®

tredition was established in 2006 by Sandra Latusseck and Soenke Schulz. Based in Hamburg, Germany, tredition offers publishing solutions to authors and publishing houses, combined with world-wide distribution of printed and digital book content. tredition is uniquely positioned to enable authors and publishing houses to create books on their own terms and without conventional manu-facturing risks.

For more information please visit: www.tredition.com

TREDITION CLASSICS

This book is part of the TREDITION CLASSICS series. The creators of this series are united by passion for literature and driven by the intention of making all public domain books available in printed format again - worldwide. Most TREDITION CLASSICS titles have been out of print and off the bookstore shelves for decades. At tredition we believe that a great book never goes out of style and that its value is eternal. Several mostly non-profit literature projects provide content to tredition. To support their good work, tredition donates a portion of the proceeds from each sold copy. As a reader of a TREDITION CLASSICS book, you support our mission to save many of the amazing works of world literature from oblivion. See all available books at www.tredition.com.

Project Gutenberg

The content for this book has been graciously provided by Project Gutenberg. Project Gutenberg is a non-profit organization founded by Michael Hart in 1971 at the University of Illinois. The mission of Project Gutenberg is simple: To encourage the creation and distribution of eBooks. Project Gutenberg is the first and largest collection of public domain eBooks.

Remarks on Clarissa (1749)

Sarah Fielding

Imprint

This book is part of TREDITION CLASSICS

Author: Sarah Fielding
Cover design: Buchgut, Berlin – Germany

Publisher: tredition GmbH, Hamburg - Germany
ISBN: 978-3-8472-1268-3

www.tredition.com
www.tredition.de

Copyright:
The content of this book is sourced from the public domain.

The intention of the TREDITION CLASSICS series is to make world literature in the public domain available in printed format. Literary enthusiasts and organizations, such as Project Gutenberg, worldwide have scanned and digitally edited the original texts. tredition has subsequently formatted and redesigned the content into a modern reading layout. Therefore, we cannot guarantee the exact reproduction of the original format of a particular historic edition. Please also note that no modifications have been made to the spelling, therefore it may differ from the orthography used today.

REMARKS

ON

CLARISSA,
Addressed to the Author.

Occasioned by some critical Conversations on the Characters and Conduct of that Work.

WITH

Some Reflections on the Character and Behaviour
of Prior's *E M M A*   .

LONDON :

Printed for *J. Robinson* in *Ludgate-street.*

M,DCC,XLIX.

[Price One Shilling.]

[2]

REMARKS

ON

CLARISSA, &c.

SIR ,

ERHAPS an Address of this Nature [3] may appear very unaccountable, and whimsical; when I assure you, my Design is fairly to lay before you all the Criticisms, as far as I can remember them, that I have heard on your History of *Clarissa*; from the Appearance of the two first Volumes, to the Close of the Work. I have not willingly omitted any one Objection I have heard made to your favourite Character, from her first Appearance in the World; nor, on the contrary, have I either diminished or added to the favourable Construction put on her Words or Actions. If the Grounds for the Objections are found to be deducible from the Story, I would have them remain in their full Force; but if the Answers her Admirers have given to those Objections are found to result from an impartial and attentive perusal of the Story, I would not have her deny'd the Justice they have done her. But tho' I seem here to speak only of *Clarissa*, as she is your principal Character, yet I intend [4] as well to take notice of what has been said relating to your whole Story, as to her in particular.

In the first Conversation I heard on this Subject, the whole Book was unanimously condemned, without the least Glimpse of Favour from any one present who sat in judgment on it. It was tedious stuff!—low!—Letters wrote between Misses about their Sweethearts!—There was an Uncle *Anthony*—a Brother *James*!—a Goody *Norton*!—and a Servant *Hannah*.—In short, *one* had no Patience to read it, *another* could not bear it, a *third* did not like it, *&c.* Such general Censurers, I knew, could be very little worth attending to; and this Judgment I should have formed had I been a Stranger to the Book thus unmercifully treated; but as I had read *Clarissa*, and observed some Beauties in it, yet heard not one of them mentioned, I was determined to say nothing, and to make my Visit as short as possible.

From hence I went to spend the Evening with a Family in whose Conversation I am always agreeably entertained. There happened, that Night, to be a pretty large Assembly of mix'd Company. *Clarissa* immediately became the Subject of our Conversation, when, after a few general Remarks, one of the Gentlemen said, "His chief Objection was to the Length of it, for that he was certain he could tell the whole Story contained in the two first Volumes in a few Minutes; for Example, (continued he) There is a Family who live in the Country, consisting of an old, positive, gouty Gentleman, two old Batchelors as positive as their gouty Brother, a meek Wife, an ambitious Son, an envious elder Sister, and a handsome younger Sister; who, having refused many offered Matches, engages the Attention and Liking of one Mr. *Lovelace*, a [5] young Gentleman of a noble Family; her Brother has an absolute Aversion to him; a Rencounter follows between them; the Lady corresponds with *Lovelace* to prevent farther Mischief; a disagreeable Man is proposed to her by all her Family; she will not consent; they all combine to insist on her Compliance; she is lock'd up; forbid all Correspondence out of the Family, but still persists in her Refusal; they call it Obstinacy; she calls it Resolution; Mr. *Lovelace* takes the Advantage of her Friends cruel Usage of her, and presses her to throw herself on his Protection: at last, for fear of being forced to marry the Man she hates, she appoints to go off with *Lovelace*; but fearing the Consequence of such a rash Step, and thinking it a Breach of her Duty to leave her Father's House till urged by the last Necessity, she would have retracted the Appointment, and waited yet a little longer, in hopes her Friends might be influenced to change their Mind; Mr. *Lovelace* does not take the Letter she puts in the usual Place for that purpose, and we see by her last Letter to her Friend, dated at St. *Albans*, that she is there with *Lovelace*. Now, how is it possible for this Story, without being exceeding tedious, to be spun out to two Volumes, containing each above 300 Pages?"

When the Gentleman ceased, a young Lady, whose Name was *Gibson*, took a little Almanack out of her Pocket, and, turning to the Place where the Births and Deaths of the Kings of *England* were marked, gave it to the Gentleman, and said, "that by his Rule of Writing, that was the best History of *England*, and Almanack-makers were the best Historians".

Mr. *Johnson*, another of the Company, said, he would engage to relate the *Roman* History, in that manner, in as little time as had been expended in the [6] summing up the Story of *Clarissa*; and then, with a Monotony in his Voice that expressed more Humour than I can describe, he began as follows:

"*Romulus* the Son of *Apulius*, as some say, tho' according to others the Son of *Mars* by one of the Vestal Virgins, built the City of *Rome*, and reign'd there 37 Years; after him reigned six Kings successively (their Names are of no Consequence) but the Wickedness of the last King put an end to the regal State, and introduced the Consular, which we may say lasted about the Space of 427 Years, tho' it was retrenched in Power by the Tribunes of the People, and had many Intermissions by the Creation of Dictators, the Decemviri, and the military Tribuns; during all this time, sometimes there was War, sometimes there was Peace, foreign Wars in abundance, great Civil Wars, not a few Contentions for Power amongst all Degrees of Men, vast Conquests, great Extent or Empire, till at last, in the famous Plains of *Pharsalia*, was fought a decisive Battel for the Empire, between two ambitious Men, namely, *Cæsar* and *Pompey*; the latter fled, and was treacherously slain on the *Egyptian* Shore, whilst the former remain'd Master of the Field, and almost of the Universe."

Here Mr. *Johnson* changed the Tone of his Voice, and said, "I will pursue this no farther, for to the Death of *Pompey* makes twenty Volumes in the History wrote by the Fathers *Catrou* and *Rouillé*, which is generally allowed to be a very good one, and, I think, one of its chief Beauties depends on the Length; for to that we owe the displaying so many various Characters, and the diving into the Motives of those great Mens Actions, who guided that extensive, powerful, I had almost said unmanagable Common-wealth. [7]

Mr. *Singleton* laugh'd, and said, "He was surprised to hear a Man of Mr. *Johnson's* Understanding display so much Eloquence to prove, (if he intended to prove any thing by it) that the knowing the Particulars of the Family at *Harlow-place* was of as much Consequence, as the knowing the Springs and Wheels on which turned the Affairs of the greatest Commonwealth that was ever heard of since the Creation of the World.

"Indeed, Sir, replied the Lady of the House, (who has bred up three Sons and three Daughters, who do Honour to her Education of them) I really think the penetrating into the Motives that actuate the Persons in a private Family, of much more general use to be known, than those concerning the Management of any Kingdom or Empire whatsoever: The latter, Princes, Governors, and Politicians only can be the better for, whilst every Parent, every Child, every Sister, and every Brother, are concerned in the former, and may take example by such who are in the same Situation with themselves.

Mr. *Clark* said, "that he believed the whole Account of the Mind of Man, were we only to mention the primary Passions, might be comprised in a few Words; but (continued he) from those Fountains to trace the several Channels into which they flow, and to get a Clue to guide us through all the winding Labyrinths into which they turn themselves, is no such easy Matter; that

> *Life's but a walking Shadow, a poor Player,*
> *That struts and frets his Hour upon the Stage*
> *And then is heard no more,*

perhaps gives us as strong an Image as it is possible to receive, of all the great Transactions perform'd by Mankind for these 6000 Years; and yet the celebrated Author, who wrote those Words, has diversify'd and display'd that strutting and fret [8] ting in as many various Lights as he has drawn Characters throughout his immortal Writings.

"In these two Volumes of *Clarissa*, it plainly appears, the Author's Intention is to impress deeply on the Reader's Mind, the peculiar Character of each Person in that Family whence his Heroine is derived; and in this I think he has succeeded so well, that for my own part I am as intimately acquainted with all the *Harlows*, as if I had known them from my Infancy; and if I was to receive a Letter from any one of them, I am sure I should not want the Name to assist me in assigning it to the proper Person. Tho', upon the whole, I don't know but there may be some Exuberances that might have been spared, as they stop the Progress of the Story, and keep us in anxious doubt concerning *Clarissa's* Fate, altho' the scattered Observations have generally the Recommendation of Novelty to amuse the Curious, Depth to engage the Attention of the Considerate, and Sprightliness to entertain the Lively; and Story is considered by the Author, as he says in his Preface, but as the Vehicle to convey the more necessary Instruction. And *Clarissa* says to Miss *How*;

You will always have me give you minute Descriptions, nor suffer me to pass by the Air and Manner in which Things are spoken, that are to be taken notice of; rightly observing, that Air and Manner often express more than the accompanying Words.

"If this Observation is just, and Air and Manner can be placed before a Reader's View by writing, I am sure minute Descriptions are necessary; and I could point out several Places in *Clarissa*, where we may see the very Look of the Eyes, and Turn of the Countenance of the Persons [9] mentioned, and hear the Tone of the Voice of the Person speaking."

The next Objection was raised by Mr. *Dobson*, to Mrs. *Harlowe's* Character, which he said, "It was plain you did not intend as a bad one, by her Meekness, Submission to her Husband, and her hitherto truly maternal Care of her Family; and yet, when she joins with violent overbearing Spirits, to oppress and persecute such a Daughter as *Clarissa*, because she steadily adhered to a Resolution of refusing solemnly to vow at the Altar Love and Obedience to such a Wretch as *Solmes*, what was this but Tameness and Folly instead of Meekness?"

Totally to justify Mrs. *Harlowe* was not attempted; on the contrary, it was unanimously agreed, that she was to blame: But Miss *Gibson* desired "Mrs. *Harlow's* Faults might not be thrown on the Author, unless it could be proved that he himself intended her Conduct should deserve no Censure. However, (continued she) to preserve any Charity in censuring her, I think it should be considered, how much a Woman must be embarassed, who has for many Years accustomed herself to obey the very Looks of another, where a Point is peremptorily insisted on, which, to comply with, must gall her to the Heart. Mrs. *Harlowe* might indeed have suffered with *Clarissa*, but could not have preserved her from her Father's Fury, irritated and inflamed by her ambitious violent Brother: And perhaps she flatter'd herself, that she might gain more Influence by seeming to comply, than if she had attempted absolutely to resist the Storm gathering in her Family. And this I think, the many Hints she gives, that if she was left to herself, it would be otherwise, is a full Proof of." [10]

A young Lady, who had hitherto been silent, looked pleased at Miss *Gibson's* Remarks, and said;

"I think *Clarissa* herself has made very good Observations on her Mamma's Meekness, and the Effects of it, in one of her Letters to Miss *Howe*, where she says—In my Mamma's Case, your Observation is verifyed, that those who will bear much, shall have much to bear. And how true is her farther Observation, where she says, that she fears her Mamma has lost that very Peace which she has sacrificed so much to obtain."

"Your Remark, Madam, said Miss *Gibson*, is very just, and from this Character of Mrs. *Harlowe*, we may draw a noble and most useful Moral; for as in the Body, too rich Blood occasions many Diseases, so in the Mind, the very Virtues themselves, if not carefully watched, may produce very hurtful Maladies. Meekness therefore, and a long Habit of Submission, is often accompanied by a want of Resolution, even where Resolution is commendable. To be all Softness, Gentleness and Meekness, and at the same time to be steadily fixed in every Point 'tis improper to give up, is peculiar to *Clarissa* herself, and a Disposition of Mind judiciously reserved by the Author for his Heroine alone."

An old Gentleman who sat in the Corner, and often made wry Faces at the sudden Attack of Rheumatick Pains, with which he was often afflicted, objected strongly to Mr. *Harlowe's* arbitrary Usage of such a Wife, as being very unnatural. "Nay, Sir, (said Miss *Gibson*) I think *Clarissa* gives a very good Account of Mr. *Harlowe's* Behaviour, in a Letter to her Friend, when she says;

But my Father was soured by the cruel Distemper I have named, which seized him all at once, in the very prime of Life, in so violent a Manner, as to take from the most active Mind, as HIS was, all Power of Activity, and that in all Appearance for Life. — It imprison'd, as I may say, his lively Spirits in himself and turned the Edge of them against his own Peace, his extraordinary Prosperity adding but to his Impatiency.

"And methinks, it is very easy to imagine, Mr. [11] *Harlowe's* Pains, and Mrs. *Harlowe's* tender Concern for these Pains increasing together: her Attention to him, and earnest Endeavours to soften and alleviate the Extremity of his Torments becoming all her Care; till, his Ill-temper daily growing stronger by the Force of his bodily Disorders, he at last habituated himself to vent it on the Person who most patiently submitted, tho' her Heart was most nearly touched and affected by it. And I appeal to the common Experience of any Persons who have accustomed themselves to make Observations on the Scenes before them, if they have not often seen heart-breaking Harshness burst forth on those who strongest feel the Strokes, and yet submit to them without complaining; and this practised even by Persons who would take it much amiss to be thought peculiarly ill-natured."

The old Gentleman, without answering Miss *Gibson,* insisted on what he had said before; and then turning to his Daughter, in a rough Voice, accompanied with a fierce Look, bid her not sit so idly, but ring the Bell, that the Servant might get a Coach, for he would go home. The young Lady, who was as submissive a Daughter as Mrs. *Harlow* was a Wife, immediately obeyed his Commands, tho' it might be read in her Countenance, that she could have wished that he would have injoined them in a milder Manner; on which her Father observed, that the Girl was always out of [12] Humour and sullen when she was employed. Indeed, Sir, said the young Lady, I love to be honoured with your Commands; I was only afraid you was angry with me. A Tear stole without her Consent from her Eyes, and at the same Time she looked at her Father with a supplicating, instead of a sullen Countenance.

As soon as the Coach came, the old Gentleman, with great Roughness, commanded his Daughter to attend him, and left us; and we could not help remarking, how much the Gentleman's Behaviour had added Weight to the Force of his Criticism.

The next Objection was raised by Mr. *Dellincourt*, who found great Fault with the Liberties you have taken with the *English* Language, and said, you had coined new Words, and printed others as if you was writing a Spelling-book, instead of relating a Story. We were all silent for a few Moments, and then Miss *Gibson* said;

"Indeed, Sir, I do not pretend to be any Judge of the Accuracy of Stile, but I beg to know, if in the writing familiar Letters, many Liberties are not allowable, which in other kinds of writing might perhaps be justly condemned: And as to the printing some of the Words with Breaks between the Syllables, it certainly makes the Painting the stronger; however, I submit this entirely to the Judgment of others. But supposing this to be a failing, surely it is a trifling one, to censure a Book severely for, in which there are so many striking Beauties to be found. But to illustrate my Thoughts on this Head, I will tell you a Story that is really true.

"A Gentleman shewed a Friend of his a Picture of a favourite Horse, drawn by the celebrated Mr. *Wooten*. The Horse was unexceptionably beautiful, and the Picture excellently drawn. His [13] Friend regarded it for some Time with great Attention: When the Gentleman (who was a Lover of Pictures, and who delighted to share his Pleasures with others) earnestly asked his Friend's Opinion of the Piece he was viewing; who, after much Consideration, with a significant Shrug of his Shoulders, and a contemptuous Toss of his Hand, said, *I don't like the Skirts of the Saddle.*"

The Application of this Story was so very plain, that the whole Company were diverted with it; and thus, Sir, I think I have sumed up all the Critisism I heard either against or in favour of your *Clarissa*, on the Publication of the two first Volumes.

The next Scene of Criticism (if I may so call it) on *Clarissa* that I was present at, was on the Publication of the two succeeding Volumes.

The same Company met, with the Addition only of one Gentleman, whom I shall call *Bellario*; his known Taste and Impartiality made all those who wished Reason instead of Prejudice might judge of the Subject before them, rejoice at his Presence. The Objections now arose so fast, it was impossible to guess where they would end. *Clarissa* herself was a Prude—a Coquet—all the Contradictions mentioned some Time ago in a printed Paper, with the Addition of many more, were laid to her Charge. She was an undutiful Daughter — too strict in her Principles of Obedience to such Parents — too fond of a Rake and a Libertine — her Heart was as impenitrable and unsusceptible of Affection, as the hardest Marble. In short, the many contradictory Faults that she was at once accused of, is almost incredible: So many, that those who had attended enough to her Character, to have an Inclination to justify her, found it difficult to know where to begin to answer such a complicated Charge. But after a [14] short Silence, Miss *Gibson* with her usual Penetration, said;

"Whenever any Person is accused of a Variety of Faults, which are plainly impossible to dwell in the same Mind, I am immediately convinced the Person so accused is innocent of them all. A Prude cannot, by an observing Eye, be taken for a Coquet, nor a Coquet for a Prude, but a good Woman may be called either, or both, according to the Dispositions of her resolved Censurers; and hence I believe we may trace the Cause, why the Characters even of those Persons who do not endeavour to wear any Disguise are so very liable to be mistaken; for Partiality or Prejudice generally sit as Judges: If the former mount the Judgment-seat, how many different Terms do we make use of to express that Goodness in another, which our own fluctuating Imaginations only have erected? If the latter, how do we vary Expressions to paint that Wickedness which we are resolve to prove inhabits the Mind we think proper to condemn?" "Nay, but (said Mr. *Dellincourt*) how are we concerned either to justify or accuse *Clarissa*? we cannot be either partial to, or prejudised against her." "I know not how it is, (replyed Miss *Gibson*) but those who dread Censure, tho' Circumspection wait on every Step, will be censured, till there no longer remains in the World any of those Dispositions that delight in inflicting that Punishment on others they see they most fear. Now, tho' *Clarissa* was not so blameably fearful of Censure, but that her first Care was to preserve the Innocence of her own Mind, and do no wrong; yet it is plain, she would very gladly have avoided incurring, as well as deserving, Reproach; and that she is treated like an intimate Acquaintance by all her [15] Readers, the Author may thank himself for. I dare say, the Authors of *Cassandra*, *Clelia*, with numberless others I could name, were never in any Danger of having their Heroines thought on, or treated like human Creatures."

Bellario, who had hitherto been silent, said, "He thought *Clarissa* could not justly be accused of any material Fault, but that of wanting Affection for her Lover; for that he was sure, a Woman whose Mind was incapable of Love, could not be amiable, nor have any of those gentle Qualities which chiefly adorn the female Character. And as to her whining after her Papa and Mamma, who had used her so cruelly, (added he) I think 'tis contemptible in her."

"But, Sir, (said Miss *Gibson*) please only to consider, first, *Clarissa* is accused of want of Love, and then in a Moment she is condemned for not being able suddenly to tear from her Bosom an Affection that had been daily growing and improving from the Time of her Birth, and this built on the greatest paternal Indulgence imaginable. Affections that have taken such deep Root, are little Treasures hoarded up in the good Mind, and cannot be torn thence without causing the strongest convulsive Pangs in the Heart, where they have been long nourished: And when they are so very easily given up as you now, Sir, seem to contend for, I confess I am very apt to suspect they have only been talked of by the Persons who can part with them with so little Pain, either from Hypocrisy, or from another very obvious Cause, namely, the using Words we are accustomed to hear, without so much as thinking of their Meaning. Such Hearts I think may be much more properly compared to the Hard [16] ness of Marble, than could that of the gentle *Clarissa*.

"There is in her Behaviour, I own, a good deal of apparent Indifference to *Lovelace*; but let her Situation and his manner of treating her be considered, and I fancy the whole will be seen in a different Light from what it may appear on the first View. She has confessed to Miss *Howe*, that she could prefer him to all the Men she ever saw; and that Friend of her Heart, to whom her very inmost Thoughts were laid open all along, pronounces her to be in Love with him. It is not from Hypocrisy that she does not confess the Charge, but from the Reason Miss *Howe* gives, when she says;

I believe you did not intend Reserve to me, for two Reasons, I believe you did not; first, because you say you did not: Next, because you have not as yet been able to convince yourself how it is to be with you; and, persecuted as you are, how so to separate the Effects that spring from the two Causes (Persecution and Love) as to give to each its particular Due.

"That *Clarissa* positively did not intend to go off with *Lovelace* when she met him, to me is very plain; nor could he have prevailed on her, had not the Terrors raised in her Mind, by apprehended Murder, almost robbed her of her Senses, and hurried her away, not knowing what she did. For the Truth of this, I appeal to that charming painted Scene, where the Reader's Mind shares *Clarissa's* Terror, and is kept in one continued Tumult til.

> [A] *The Steeds are smote, the rapid Chariot flies,*
> *The sudden Clouds of circling Dust arise.*

"She was vexed to her soul afterwards to find [17] she was tricked, as she calls it, out of herself, when *Lovelace*, instead of comforting and assuring her Mind, begins such a Train of shufling artful Tricks, as no one but *Lovelace* could have thought on: And altho' she did not know all his Design, for if she had, she would certainly have left him, yet she sees enough of his *crooked ways*, to be convinced that he acted ungenerously by her, because she was in *his Power*. Does not *Lovelace*, in a Letter to *Belford*, writ in four Days after she was with him, say?

And do I not see, that I shall want nothing but Patience, in order to have all Power with me? For what shall we say, if all these Complaints of a Character Wounded, these Declarations of increasing Regrets of meeting me, of Resentments never to be got over for my seducing her away, these angry Commands to leave her, — what shall we say, if all were to mean nothing but Matrimony? — And what if my forbearing to enter upon that Subject comes out to be the true Cause of her Petulance and Uneasiness.

"And then he gives such an Account of his asking her Consent to marry him, and at the same Time artfully confusing her, so as to prevent her Consent, as perfectly paints his cunning vile Heart. How is her Behaviour altered to him from the Time she can write Miss *Howe* word that her Prospects are mended, till his returning Shufling convinces her there is no Confidence to be placed in him! But if, Sir, you cannot think *Lovelace's* Usage of *Clarissa* a full Justification of her in this Point, I think the Author has a just Right to be heard out before his Heroine is condemned in so heavy a Charge, as that of being void of all Affection. You know enough of my Sentiments, Sir, to be convinced that I do think [18] this the heaviest Charge a Woman can be accused of; for Love is the only Passion I should wish to be harboured in the gentle Bosom of a good Woman. Ambition, with all the Train of turbulent Passions the World is infested with, I would leave to Men: And could I make my whole Sex of my Opinion, they would be resigned without the least Grudge or Envy; for Peace and Harmony dwell not with them, but on the contrary, Discord, Perturbation and Misery are their constant Companions. But tho' I speak thus with the utmost Sincerity of Love; yet I cannot think a Woman greatly the Object of Esteem who, like *Serina* in the *Orphan*, having such a Father as *Acasto*, and such Brothers, affectionate to her, however blameable in other Respects; while she saw her whole Family distressed and confused, and *Monimia*, the gentle Companion of her Infancy, involved in that Confusion, her Lover too behaving like a Mad-man, yet still, could cry out,

> Chamont's *the dearest thing I have on Earth;*
> *Give me* Chamont, *and let the World forsake me.*

"*Clarissa* would have acted a different Part, I do confess; and yet, if I can guess any Thing of the Author's Intention by what is already published, I fancy, when we have read the Conclusion of this Story, we shall be convinced that Love was the strongest Characteristic of *Clarissa's* Mind."

Bellario answered, with that Candor, which is known to be one of the most distinguishing Marks of his Character by all who have the Pleasure of his Acquaintance, 'That if it proved so, he should have the greatest Esteem and highest Veneration [19] for *Clarissa*, and would suspend his Judgment till he saw the remaining Part of the Story.'

But all the Company were not so candid, for Mr. *Dellincourt* said, 'He was sure *Clarissa* could not in the remaining Part of the Story convince him, that her Characteristic was Love; for nothing less than the lovely *Emma's* Passion for *Henry* would be any Satisfaction to him, if he was a Lover.'—Miss *Gibson* said. 'She had often been sorry that the Poem of *Henry* and *Emma* had not been long ago buried in Oblivion; for (continued she) it is one of those Things which, by the Dress and Ornaments of fine Language and smooth Poetry, has imposed on Mankind so strong a Fallacy, as to make a Character in itself most despicable, nay I may say most blameable, generally thought worthy Admiration and Praise: For strip it of the dazzling Beauties of Poetry, and thus fairly may the Story be told.

An old *English* Baron retired in his Decline of Life to his Country-seat, where one only Daughter (left him by a Wife he fondly loved) was the Care, the Joy, the Comfort of his declining Years: No sooner had the State of blooming Youth taken place of that of prattling Infancy, than she became the Object of publick Admiration, and Lovers of all Degrees with Emulation strove to gain the fair *Emma's* Favour; but as yet her Heart was free, and her Father's paternal tender Indulgence never once endeavoured to force her Choice. At last the happy *Henry* in various Disguises found the means to obtain her Favour, and she becomes passionately in Love with him: But not content with this, he resolves on a Trial of her Constancy, and therefore tells her, that he is a Murderer, must fly from Justice, and herd amongst the lowest and basest of Mankind; that [20] he despised her, and the fond Heart she had given him; a younger and fairer Nymph now engaging his Pursuit, and that if she would follow him, she also must herd with Outlaws his Companions, who like himself were fled from Justice; where Impiety, Blasphemy and Obscenity would be all the Language she could hear.

Emma on this Trial, ignorant who *Henry* was, or what Brothel had last given him up, without one Enquiry whether the Murder he confessed was not of the blackest Die, remorseless for all the Agonies with which she must tear her Father's tender Bosom, resolves at all Events, as *Henry* himself says,

> *Name, Habit, Parents, Woman, left behind.*

to follow him through the World; not admitted to share his Fate, but to be scorned and insulted by him. Thus *victoriously* she stood her Trial. *Henry* turns out a great Man; consequently his Wife is greatly admired; Success crowns all, and both Grandeur and Love join to reward her supposed heroic Virtue.

But had the Poet thought proper, that *Henry* should have turned out the Murderer, the Vagabond, the insolent and ungrateful Scorner of her Love he represented himself to be; had her Father's Sorrow for her Fate shortned his miserable Days; had she been abandoned by the Wretch she had so much Reason to expect the worst of Treatment from, and, between Rage, Despair, and a thousand conflicting Passions, been led by a natural Gradation from one Vice to another, till she had been lost in the most abandoned Profligacy; instead of being proposed for an Example, her Name would have been only mentioned to deter others from the like [21] rash Steps. That this was the natural Consequence of her Actions is very apparent: Nor do I think from her Behaviour, that *Henry* had the least Reason to be convinced that she would not leave him for the first Man who would try to seduce her, provided the Colour of his Complexion suited her Fancy.

All the Company were very inclineable to yield up *Emma's* Cause, if *Henry had* indeed been a Villain and a Murderer; only great Part of them were very apt to forget one Circumstance, namely, that it was impossible for her to know, but that he was the Wretch he represented himself to be; and Miss *Gibson* seemed to be much more inclined to compassionate her, if extreme Misery had been her Fate, than was the Gentleman who first mentioned her as an Object of Admiration, only because the Author of the Poem thought fit to reward her. Miss *Gibson* then addressing herself to *Bellario*, said, 'Sir, you are a Father, — an indulgent Father, — would you have your Daughter act in such a Manner? — *Bellario* honestly owned he would not. 'Why then, Sir, (replyed she) please to consider a Moment, and you will see the Injustice of wishing another Man's Daughter should act so.' *Bellario* ingenuously confessed, that when he read the Poem of *Henry* and *Emma*, the Picture of his Mistress, and not that of his Daughter, was before his Eyes, and he would have his Mistress *of all Mankind love but him alone.* — — 'I wonder not at that, Sir, (said Miss *Gibson*) but then you would not be the Man *Henry* represented himself to be. Had *Henry* had any Misfortunes by which his Heart had not been stained.

[B] *Had it pleased Heav'n*
To try him *with Affliction, had he rain'd*
All kind of Sores and Shames on his *bare Head,*
Steep'd him *in Poverty to the very Lips,*
Given to Captivity him *and* his *utmost Hopes,*

no one would more have applauded *Emma's* Resolution, [22] *of loving of all Mankind but him alone*, than I should have done: But yet when I see a Woman seriously endeavour to conquer a Passion for a Man who proves himself unworthy her Love, it will always be to me a strong Proof of her steady Constancy to a Man she has Reason to esteem. I would have had *Emma* stood *Henry's* shocking Tryal as *Macduff* in the Tragedy of *Macbeth* does that of *Malcolm*, and when he had proved himself unworthy her least Affection; I think, in the Words of *Macduff* she might have said,

    − − Fare thee well,
These Evils thou repeat'st upon thyself,
Have banish'd me from Joy. *− −Oh! my Breast,*
Thy Hope ends here.

On such a Behaviour, I think the Reward she met with should have been founded, and such I believe would have been the Behaviour of *Clarissa* in the like Circumstances.

'The Love that is not judicious, must be as uncertain as its capricious Foundation: But 'tis one of the distinguishing Marks of *Clarissa's* Character, to watch her own Mind, that Prejudice may not get Possession of it, nor her Imagination run away with her Judgment. With what a noble Contempt does she treat the extravagant Offers *Solmes* makes her, at the Expence of Justice, and cruelly leaving his Family to starve? But how very few People, like *Clarissa*, can poise the Scales with an even [23] Hand, where one Grain of Self is placed in either Scale?'

The Gentleman, who had at first started the Objection to *Clarissa* of her being incapable of any strong Affection, now said, 'that he could not see any Proof of her Impartiality, in that she could view the Actions of *Solmes* in the proper Light: He did not know whether she would have argued in the same manner With regard to *Lovelace*'. Miss *Gibson* said, 'Do you speak this, Sir, as a Proof of the Justice of your first Objection to *Clarissa*, that her Heart was as impenetrable as Marble; is it reasonable she should be condemned both ways?' The Gentleman look'd very grave for a Moment, and then said, he was sure she had no Affections in her, notwithstand what he had now said.

Mr. *Johnson* on this, told the following Story.

"I remember (said he) I went some time ago with Mr. *Tonson* to a celebrated Painter's, to see a Picture he had drawn of a Gentleman we were both intimately acquainted with; the Resemblance was very strong; we were much pleased with the Picture, even to the very Drapery; the Coat was a fine Crimson Cloth, but Mr. *Tonson*, at first View, took it for Velvet; he was soon convinced of his Mistake, but yet could never since mention the Picture, without talking of the Velvet Coat; and when I have bid him remember it was Cloth, he has always acknowledged it, and said, it's very true Sir; And yet such a strong Impression had his first Idea of it made in his Mind, that in two Minutes he could talk again of the Velvet Coat, with as much Ease as if he had been perfectly ignorant of his Mistake."

A strong Objection was raised to Mr. *Lovelace's* being so long without any Attempt on the Lady's Honour, when she was under the same Roof with [24] him, and so much in his Power. Mr. *Johnson* said he thought Mr. *Belford* had given a good Reason for this Delay in a Letter to *Lovelace*, where he says,

Thou too a Man born for Intrigue, full of Invention, intrepid, remorseless, able patiently to watch for the Opportunity, not flurried, as most Men, by Gusts of violent Passion, which often nip a Project in the Bud, and make the Snail, which was just putting out its Horns to meet the Inviter, withdraw into its Shell.

So that it seems to be a Maxim, amongst *Lovelace* and his Club of Rakes, not to destroy their own Schemes by a too precipitate Pursuit; and *Lovelace* gives yet a stronger Reason for it in the following Words.

O Virtue, Virtue, says he, *what is there in thee, that can thus affect the Heart of such a Man as me against my Will! — Whence these involuntary Tremors, and fear of giving mortal Offence! What art thou that, acting in the Breast of a feeble Woman, canst strike so much awe into a Spirit so intrepid which never before, no, not in my first Attempt, young as I then was, and frighted at my own Boldness (till I found myself* forgiven,*) had such an Effect on me.*

But Quotations from *Lovelace's* Words to this Purpose, and that he was resolved to be slow in order to be sure, would be endless.

This, I think, was the last Objection raised; only *Bellario* said, that the Report that the Catastrophy was to be unhappy had made a deep Impression on him; for that he could not avoid thinking that, if it was true, it must be a great Error, and destroy all the Pleasure a good-natur'd Reader might already have received: However, he said, he would keep his Word in not absolutely giving his Judgment till he saw the Conclusion.

And thus ended the second Scene of Criticism on *Clarissa*; only, as we went down Stairs, a [25] Lady, who had not spoke one Word the whole Evening, mutter'd out a strong Dislike, that the agreeable Mr. *Lovelace* should not become a Husband.

And now, in the Month of *December*, appears the long expected, much wished for Conclusion of *Clarissa's* Story.

The Company we have already mentioned being again assembled, the Lady who had before grieved that the agreeable Mr. *Lovelace* should not become a Husband, now lamented that Miss *Howe* should be married to so insipid a Man (that was the Epithet she chose for him) as Mr. *Hickman*. This passed some little time without any Answer. Miss *Gibson* was silent; and I saw by her Looks that she thought there was some Weight in her Objection. At last an old Lady, who had three Daughters marriagable, said, she wondered to hear Mr. *Hickman* called insipid; for she thought there could be no Reason for giving him that Appellation, unless young Women would confess what she should be very sorry to hear them confess, namely, that, in their Opinion, Sobriety intitles a Man to the Character of Insipidity. Pray remember, continued the Lady, that there is no Ridicule cast upon Mr. *Hickman* throughout the whole Story, but by *Lovelace* and Miss *Howe*. The former lov'd Ridicule so well, that he could make Objects of it, by the Help of his gay Imagination, even where he found none: Besides, he hated any Man should have a fine Woman but himself; for, in his Opinion, he alone deserved them. And I think Miss *Howe* is very censurable for the Liberties she takes with a worthy Man, whom also it is plain she intends to make her Husband.

Miss *Gibson* agreed in censuring Miss *Howe* for the Liberties she takes with him; but at the same time said, she thought even his bearing that Usage did lower his Character. Now you see, replied the Lady, [26] how you are taken in; that you can condemn Miss *Howe* for her Contempt of Mr. *Hickman*, and yet at the same time let the lively Strokes that fall from her Pen have their full force against the abused worthy Man. Yet Miss *Howe* herself owns, as early as the second Volume, that Mr. *Hickman* is humane, benevolent, generous, — No Fox-hunter — No Gamester — That he is sober, modest, and virtuous; and has Qualities that Mothers would be fond of in a Husband for their Daughters; and for which, perhaps, their Daughters would be the happier, could they judge as well for themselves as Experience may teach them to judge for their future Daughters. In other Places he is represented as charitable, considerate to Inferiors, so obliging and respectful to his Mother-in-law, that she leaves him at her Death, in Acknowledgment of it, all that was in her Power: And Miss *Howe* owns he never disobliged her by Word or Look. What then is the Objection to Mr. *Hickman*? Why truly, he has not *Lovelace's* fine Person! — *Lovelace's* fine Address! — *Lovelace's* impetuous Spirit; and yet he has shewn even *Lovelace*, that he wants not Courage. He is plain in his Dress! — His Gait shews him not to be so debonnaire in dancing a Minuit as *Lovelace*. — But, indeed, I am afraid whoever prefers a *Lovelace* to a *Hickman*, will wish all her lifetime she could have sooner found out, that tho' *Lovelace* was the best Partner at a Ball; yet, when a Companion for Life was to be chose, that Mr. *Hickman's* Goodness of Heart rendered him in all respects more essential to Happiness; much more eligible than all the gay, fluttering, and parading Spirit of a *Lovelace* could possibly have done. And your Favourite *Clarissa*, Miss *Gibson*, says in a Letter to

Miss *Howe*; 'Will you never, my Dear, give the Weight which you, and all our Sex ought to give to the Qualities of So [27] briety and Regularity of Life and Manners in that Sex?—Must bold Creatures and forward Spirits for ever, and by the wisest and best of us, as well as by the indiscretest, be the most kindly used?—be best thought of'?

Again, in her posthumous Letter—'Your Choice is fallen upon a sincere, an honest, a virtuous, and what is more than all, a *pious Man.*—A Man who altho' he admires your Person, is still more in love with the Graces of your Mind; and as those Graces are improvable with every added Year of Life, which will impair the transitory ones of Person, what a firm Basis has Mr. *Hickman* chosen to build his Love upon.'

The same Man cannot be every thing: A *Hickman* in Heart, to a *Lovelace* in Vivacity and Address, perhaps, is almost impossible to be met with; Time, Opportunities, and Inclinations are wanting.

Nay, Madam, says Miss *Gibson*, I do not dispute Mr. *Hickman's* being preferable for a Husband to Mr. *Lovelace*; the Heart is certainly the first thing to be considered in a Man to whose Government a Woman resigns herself; but I should not chuse either *Lovelace* or *Hickman*. I must confess I should desire Humour and Spirit in a Man. A married Life, tho' it cannot be said to be miserable with an honest Husband; yet it must be very dull, when a Man has not the Power of diversifying his Ideas enough to display trifling Incidents in various Lights; and 'tis impossible where this is wanting, but that a Man and his Wife must often depend on other Company to keep them from sinking into Insipidity. And for my part, I cannot paint to myself any thing more disagreeable, than to sit with a Husband and wish some-body would come in and relieve us from one another's Dulness. Trifles, Madam, become strong Entertainments to sprightly Minds! [28] —

Ah! Miss *Gibson*, replied the Lady, in every Word you speak, you prove how necessary the Author's Moral is to be strongly inculcated; when even *your* serious and thoughtful Turn of Mind will not suffer you to see through the Glare of what you call Humour and Spirit with that Clearness which would enable you to distinguish how very seldom that Humour and Spirit is bestowed on a Wife.

Mr. *Hickman's* whole Mind being at Home, would enliven him into a chearful Companion with his Wife; whilst a *Lovelace's* Mind, engaged on foreign Objects, would often make him fall into Peevishness and Ill-humour, instead of this so much dreaded *Insipidity*.

Indeed, Madam, said Miss *Gibson*, I don't plead for Mr. *Lovelace*; for I detest him of all the Men I ever read of.

That is true, replied the Lady; but that is because you have *read* of him, and know the Villanies he was capable of. But yet, I think, you have plainly proved, if a *Lovelace* and a *Hickman* contended for your Favour, which would have the best Chance of succeeding.

Miss *Gibson* blushed, and was silent; when a sprightly Girl, of about Sixteen, said, She loved Mr. *Hickman* very much; he was a good, and a gentle-hearted Man—But indeed she should not like him for her Husband.

The Gentlemen, during this Debate, had all sat silent; but they often smiled to see how few Advocates Mr. *Hickman* was likely to have amongst the Ladies.

At last *Bellario* said, If I had not thought so before, I should now be convinced by this Conversation, how judicious the Author of *Clarissa* was in setting forth so very strongly as he does, the Necessity of Sobriety and Goodness in a Husband, in or [29] der to render a married State happy. For you have shown clearly, Ladies, how difficult it is for a Man to be esteemed by you who has those Qualities, since I can see no one Objection to Mr. *Hickman*, but that he has not that Gaiety of Disposition which from a vast Flow of animal Spirits, without Restraint or Curb from either Principles of Religion or Good-nature, shines forth in *Lovelace's* wild Fancies. And this Man you find such a Reluctance to speak well of; tho' a reforming *Belford* esteems; Colonel *Morden* highly values him; and says, he is respected by all the World!—And a *Clarissa* for ever acknowledges his Merit.—And, in one of the last Actions of her Life, praises him as he deserves to be praised. And earnestly recommends it to her best and dear Friend, to give both her Hand and Heart to so worthy a Man. The steady Principles of Mr. *Hickman* was a firm Basis to depend on, for Protection and good Usage.

Miss *Gibson* was so much pleased with seeing *Bellario* enter so heartily into the Design of the Author of *Clarissa,* that she dropp'd the Argument, (tho' she did not seem quite convinc'd that Mr. *Hickman* could be an agreeable Husband) and with some Earnestness desired *Bellario* to tell her, whether he was not now convinced that *Clarissa* was capable of the strongest Affection, could she but have found the least Foundation to have built that Affection on: Yes, replied *Bellario,* I am convinced of it, and am surprised that I did not before see how much *Lovelace's* base unmanly Behaviour justifies her in this Point; he himself, indeed, in the Letter he writes *Belford* after he left *England,* lays the whole Scene before us; to his own Condemnation, and *Clarissa's* eternal Honour: He owns her meek and gentle Spirit; confesses he repeatedly, from the first, poured cold Water on her rising Flame, by meanly and in [30] gratefully turning upon her the Injunctions which Virgin Delicacy, and filial Duty induced her to lay him under before he got her into his Power; he quotes her own Words: *That she could not be guilty of Affectation or Tyranny to the Man she intended to marry;* that from the Time he had got her from her Father's House, *he had a plain Path before him;* that *he had held her Soul in suspense an Hundred times;* that *she would have had no Reserves, had he not given her Cause of Doubt;* that she owned to *Belford,* that *once she could have loved him; and could she have made him Good would have made him Happy.*

To this Letter, continued *Bellario,* and numerous other Places in the Book, would I refer all those, if any such there are, who yet doubt her being capable of Love. Surely we may fairly conclude with *Lovelace,* that well might she, who had been used to be courted and admired by every desiring Eye, and worshipped by every respectful Heart—Well might such a Woman be allowed to draw back, when she found herself kept in suspence, as to the great Question of all, by a designing and intriguing Spirit, pretending Awe and Distance, as Reasons for reining in a Fervour, which, if real, cannot be reined in.

Clarissa seems indeed, as Colonel *Morden* says, (added the now-admiring *Bellario*) to have been, as much as Mortal could be, LOVE ITSELF.

Miss *Gibson* was highly delighted with what *Bellario* said, and added to it, That she thought *Clarissa's* frankness of Heart was very apparent, from the manner in which she had treated those Gentlemen her Heart had obliged her to refuse, and from the generous Advice she in so many Places gives Miss *Howe*, in relation to her Treatment of Mr. *Hickman*: And pray, Sir, continued Miss *Gibson*, pardon my asking you one Question more, namely; whether you are not [31] now satisfied with the Conduct of the Author in the Management of his whole Story?

Bellario answered, That he was not only satisfied with it, but highly applauded all the material Parts of it; that the various distressful Situations in which you had placed your Heroine, were noble beyond Expression; that these three last Volumes contained many Scenes, each singly arising to as high a Tragedy as can possibly be wrote; that the Tears you had drawn from his Eyes were such Tears as flow'd from a Heart at once filled with Admiration and Compassion, and labouring under Sensations too strong for any Utterance in Words; and that for the Sake of *Clarissa*, he would never form any Judgment of a Work again till the whole was lain before him. This was noble! this was candid! this was like *Bellario*! and Miss *Gibson* could not forbear saying, that she rejoyced in the Tears *he* had shed for *Clarissa*. And, Sir, (continued she) 'I am convinced, that those whose Eyes melt not at Scenes of well-wrought Distress, cannot properly be said to laugh, from a liberal and chearful Spirit, at the true Scenes of comic Humour.'

'The Beginning of this Season I went with a Lady, whose Acquaintance I accidentally fell into, to *Drury-Lane* Play-house, where Mr. *Garrick* performed the Part of King *Lear*. I should have thought (tho' altered and defaced as it is by Mr. *Tate*) that even Butchers must have wept; but to my great Astonishment, my Companion sat unmoved: Silent indeed she was, only now and then said, *she did not love Tragedy*; that, for her part, *she had rather laugh than cry*, and liked a Comedy best. I had a Curiosity to see in what manner comic Scenes would affect her; and therefore proposed going to *Covent-Garden* Play-house the next Night, when Mr. *Quin* was to play the Part [32] of Sir *John Falstaff*, in *Harry* the Fourth. Accordingly we went. The Lady did, indeed, now and then catch the Laugh of those around her, enough to move about her Features a little; but upon the whole, was pretty near as unmov'd as she had been the Night before; and at last she confessed, that the Humours of Sir *John Falstaff* was not the Sort of Comedy that pleased her Fancy; but that the merry Dialogues between *Tom* and *Phillis* in the *Conscious Lovers*, and the comical Humours of *Ben* and Miss *Prue* in *Love for Love*, were more suited to her Taste. I was not much surprised, because I before suspected, that whoever could sit the Play of King *Lear* without weeping, would see Sir *John Falstaff* without laughing.'

Mr. *Dellincourt* now raised a new Objection to *Clarissa*, in that she talked so much of Religion, which he call'd Canting. Nay, Sir, said *Bellario*, 'I cannot see how she can be said to cant; for her religious Reflections are neither nonsensical or affected, but such as naturally arise from a pious Mind in her several Situations; and if you are a Christian, Sir, I am sure you cannot, on Consideration, dislike that Part of her Character.' Mr. *Dellincourt* said, 'Yes, he was a Christian, and he did not dislike some of her Reflections, at least when she was near Death; but he thought she talked too much of Religion at the Beginning; for it was unnatural for a young Beauty to have such grave Thoughts.' *Bellario* smiled and said,

'You put me in mind, Sir, of Dame *Quickly*, who when Sir *John Falstaff*, in his Illness, calls upon God, told him, to comfort him, she hoped there was no Occasion yet to think of any such Matters; supposing, that to think of God, except he was quite dying, was very unnecessary. And, indeed, I have often known a professed Christian excuse introducing a Word of Religion into Com [33] pany, as if it would be indecent to mention any such matters; but as to *Clarissa*, I think the Principles she had imbibed from her Infancy from the good and pious Mrs. *Norton*, and which were afterwards strengthned by her Conversation with Doctor *Lewin*, renders it very natural for her to be early and steadily religious.' Mr. *Dellincourt* made no Answer, but dropped his Objection; and Mr. *Barker* said, 'that he thought there was one great Fault in the Conduct of your Story; and that was, the Indelicacy of making *Clarissa* seek *Lovelace* after the Outrage; for that he was strongly of Opinion, that she had better have escaped from Mrs. *Sinclair's* and have avoided the Sight of *Lovelace*.' 'Indeed, Sir, said Miss *Gibson*, I believe she would have been very thankful for your Advice, if you could at the same time have found out any Expedient to have put it in Execution; but if you will please to recollect, you may remember the Difficulty she had to escape once before, even when she was not suspected; and *Lovelace* now could have no manner of doubt, but that she would fly that House, if not prevented, as soon as her Strength would permit her to leave her Bed.

As to the Indelicacy of *Clarissa's* seeking *Lovelace*, said *Bellario*, 'I confess I do not see it; however, I will leave that matter to be decided by the Ladies', who all agreed, that they thought it no Breach of the strictest Modesty to declare it was their Opinion, that the whole Scene, as it now stands, is what it *should be*, and would have admited of no Alteration, but for the worse; that the picturesque Manner in which a young Woman, without Fear or Confusion, beholds the Man who dared imagine his Guilt could baffle all her Resolutions, and sink her Soul to Cowardice, most beautifully displays the Power of conscious Innocence; and, on the other hand, that the [34] confused Mind, the flattering Speech, unavoidable even by a *Lovelace* when his guilty Soul was awed by the Presence of an Object injured beyond the Power of Reparation, displays the Deformity of Wickedness in all its Force. In short, this Scene was allowed to be Virtue's Triumph, and *Clarissa's* Conduct to be a direct Opposition to that of all those whining Women, who blubber out an humble Petition to be joined for Life to the Men who have betrayed them.

Had not *Clarissa* seen *Lovelace*, said Miss *Gibson*, her Triumph could never have been so compleat; and as I think the Impossibility of her Escape at that time, from Mrs. *Sinclair's*, is very apparent, had she not sought him, the true Lovers of *Clarissa* must have mourned the Loss of seeing her Behaviour in such an uncommon Situation.

Bellario gave these Sentiments a Sanction by his Approbation, and the rest of the Company either concurr'd with his Opinion, or at least did not contradict him; and the next Day Miss *Gibson* received the following Letter from *Bellario*.

MADAM ,

Y OU seem'd so pleased last Night with my Conversion, if I may be allowed the Expression, to your Favourite *Clarissa*, that I could not seek any Repose till I had thrown together my Thoughts on that Head, in order to address them to you; nor am I ashamed to confess, that the Author's Design is more noble, and his Execution of it much happier, than I even suspected till I had seen the whole.

In a Series of familiar Letters to relate a compleat Story, where there is such a Variety of Characters, every one conducing to the forming the necessary Incidents to the Completion of that Story, is a Method so intirely new, so much an Original manner [35] of Writing, that the Author seems to have a Right to make his own Laws; the painting Nature is indeed his Aim, but the Vehicle by which he conveys his lively Portraits to the Mind is so much his own Invention, that he may guide and direct it according to his own Will and Pleasure. *Aristotle* drew his Rules of Epic Poetry from *Homer*, and not *Homer* from *Aristotle*; tho' had they been Cotemporaries, perhaps that had been a Point much disputed.

As to the Length of the Story, I fancy that Complaint arises from the great Earnestness the Characters inspire the Reader with to know the Event; and on a second Reading may vanish. *Clarissa* is not intended as a Dramatic, but as a real Picture of human Life, where Story can move but slowly, where the Characters must open by degrees, and the Reader's own Judgment form them from different Parts, as they display themselves according to the Incidents that arise. As for Example; the Behaviour of *Lovelace* to his Rosebud must strike every one, at first View, with Admiration and Esteem for him; but when his Character comes to blaze in its full Light, it is very apparent that his Pride preserved his Rosebud, as well as it destroyed *Clarissa*; like *Milton's Satan*, he could for a Time cloath himself like an Angel of Light, even to the Deception of *Uriel*.

> *For neither Man, nor Angel can discern*
> *Hypocrisie; the only Evil that walks*
> *Invisible, except to God alone,*
> *By his permissive Will, through Heaven and Earth:*
> *And oft, though Wisdom wake, Suspicion sleeps*
> *At Wisdom's Gate, and to Simplicity*
> *Resigns her Charge; while Goodness thinks no ill*
> *Where no Ill seems; which now, for once, beguiled*
> Uriel, *though Regent of the Sun, and held*
> *The sharpest-sighted Spirit of all in Heaven.*

Proud Spirits, such as *Satan's* and *Lovelace's*, require [36] Objects of their Envy, as Food for their Malice, to compleat their Triumph and applaud their own Wickedness. From this Incident of the Rose-bud, and the subsequent Behaviour of *Lovelace*, arises a Moral which can never be too often inculcated; namely, that Pride has the Art of putting on the Mask of Virtue in so many Forms, that we must judge of a Man upon the whole, and not from any one single Action.

A celebrated *French* Critick says, that

'An indifferent Wit may form a vast Design in his Imagination; but it must be an Extraordinary Genius that can work his Design, and fashion it according to Justness and Proportion: For 'tis necessary that the same Spirit *reign throughout*; that all contribute to the same *End*; and that all the *Parts* bear a secret *Relation* to each other; all depend on this Relation and Alliance.'

Let the nicest Critick examine the Story of *Clarissa*, and see if in any Point it fails of coming up exactly to the before-mentioned Rule. The Author had all Nature before him, and he has beautifully made use of every Labyrinth, in the several Minds of his Characters, to lead him to his purposed End.

The Obstinacy of old *Harlowe*, who never gave up a Point, unaccustomed to Contradiction, and mad with the Thoughts of his own Authority; the Pride of the two old Batchelors, who had lived single, in order to aggrandize their Family; the overbearing impetuous *James Harlowe's* Envy, arising from Ambition; the two-fold Envy of *Arabella Harlowe*, springing from Rivalship in general Admiration, as well as in particular liking; the former more rough, the latter more sly, tho' full as keen in her Reproaches; the constant Submission of Mrs. [37] *Harlowe*, and the mad Vanity of *Lovelace*, all conspire to the grand End of distressing and destroying the poor *Clarissa*; whose Misfortune it was to be placed amongst a Set of Wretches, who were every one following the Bent of their own peculiar Madness, without any Consideration for the innocent Victim who was to fall a Sacrifice to their ungovernable Passions. And here I must observe, how artfully the Author has conducted the opening of his different Characters, as they became more interested in his Story. The Correspondence between Miss *Howe* and *Clarissa*, with some characteristical Letters of each of the *Harlowes*, as these were then his principal Actors, chiefly compose the two first Volumes.

In the third, fourth and fifth Volumes, *Lovelace* comes prancing before the Reader's Eye; gives an unrestrained Loose to his uncurbed Imagination, and ripens into full-blown Baseness that Blackness of Mind, which had hitherto only shot forth in Buds but barely visible. The strong and lively Pen of *Lovelace* was most proper to relate the most active Scenes. But when his mischievous Heart and plotting Head had left him no farther use for his wild Fancies, than to rave and curse his own Folly, *Belford* takes up the Pen, and carries on the Story; and in the sixth and seventh Volumes, Colonel *Morden* (who has hitherto made but a small Appearance) is brought upon the Stage, and his Character, as he is to be the Instrument of the Death of *Lovelace*, is as strongly painted, and as necessary to the Completion of the Story, as are any of the others. It is astonishing to me how much the different Stile of each Writer is in every Particular preserved; indeed so characteristically preserved, that when I read *Clarissa's* Letters, where every Line speaks the considerate and the pious Mind, I could almost think the Author [38] had studied nothing but her Character. When Miss *Howe's* lively Vein and flowing Wit entertains me, She appears to have been the principal Person in his Thoughts. When Mrs. *Harlowe* writes, her broken half-utter'd Sentences are so many Pictures of the broken timorous Spirit of Meekness tyrannised over, that dictates to her Pen. When Mr. *Harlowe* condescends to sign his much valued Name, the dictatorial Spirit of an indulged tyrannic Disposition indites every arbitrary Command. When *John Harlowe* writes, the Desire of proving himself of Consequence from his Fortune, and being infected with the Idea of his Niece's Disobedience, (a Word which continually resounded through his Family) plainly appear to be the only two Causes that make him insist on her Compliance. In *Anthony Harlowe's* Roughness and Reproaches, 'The Sea prosper'd Gentleman, (as *Clarissa* says) not used to any but elemental Controul, and even ready to buffet that, blusters as violently as the Winds he was accustomed to be angry at.' In *James Harlowe's* Letters, we see how the Mind infected with the complicated Distemper of Envy, Insolence and Malice, can blot the fair Paper, and poison it with its Venom. In *Arabella Harlowe*, the sly Insinuations of feminine Envy break forth in every taunting Word, and she could "speak Daggers, tho' she dared not use them." But, to imitate our Author, in turning suddenly from this detestable Picture, how does every Line of the good Mrs. *Norton* shew us a Mind inured to, and patiently submitting to Adversity, looking on Contempt as the unavoidable Consequence of Poverty, and fixed in a firm and pious Resolution of going through all the Vicissitudes of this transitory Life without repining.

Nor does the Author fail more in the preserving [39] the characteristical Difference of Stile in the Writings of *Mowbray*, *Belford* and *Lovelace*.

Mowbray, tho' he writes but two Letters in the whole, yet do those two so strongly fix his Character, that every Reader may see of what Consequence he made himself to Society; namely, to act the blustring Part in a Club of Rakes, to fill a Seat at the Table, and assist in keeping up the Roar and Noise necessary to make the Life of such Assemblies.

Mr. *Belford's* Letters prove, that he acts the second Part under Mr. *Lovelace*; he follows the Paths the other beats through the thorny Labyrinths of wild Libertinism; he has not the lively Humour of *Lovelace*, altho' in Understanding I think he has rather the Advantage; and his not being quite so lively, is owing to his not giving such a loose to every unbridled Fancy; but he has less Pride, and consequently more Humanity: this appears in the many Arguments he makes use of to his Friend in favour of *Clarissa*; but these Arguments, as they are only the Produce of sudden Starts of Compassion, and have no fixed Principle for their Basis, could have no Weight with *Lovelace*; and the fluctuating of a Mind sometimes intruded upon by the Force of Good-nature, and then again actuated by the Principles of Libertinism, is finely set before us by *Belford's* Writings. And as there is a great Beauty throughout the whole of *Clarissa*, in the specific Difference of Stile preserved by every Writer, so is there an inimitable Beauty in *Belford* differing from himself, when he changes the State of his Mind; his Stile accompanies that Change, and he appears another Man. He was always more of the true Gentleman in his Stile than *Lovelace*, because his Will was not enough overbearing to break through all Bounds; but when his Mind is softned by the many different Deaths he is witness of, and he becomes animated by *Clarissa's* [40] Example to think in earned of reforming his Life, the Gentleman and the Christian increase together, till he becomes at once the Executor of *Clarissa's* Will, and, if I may be allowed the Expression, the Heir to her Principles.

In *Lovelace's* Stile, his Humour, his Parts, his Pride, his wild Desire of throwing Difficulties in his own way, in order to conquer them, and exercise his own intriguing Spirit, break forth in every Line. His impetuous Will, unrestrained from his Infancy, as he himself complains, by his Mother, and long accustomed to bear down all before it, destroys the Gentleman, and equally every other amiable Qualification: For tho' a Knowledge of the Customs of the World may make a Man in Company, where he stays but a little while, appear polite; yet when that Man indulges himself in gratifying continually his own wild Humour, those who are intimate with him, must often have Cause to complain of his Unpoliteness; as *Clarissa* does of *Lovelace*. And by such Complaints of *Clarissa*, I think it is very apparent, that the Author designed *Lovelace* should be unpolite, notwithstanding his Station, in order to prove that indulged overbearing Passions will trample under Foot every Bar that would stop them in their raging Course. But now I am upon the Subject of the different Stiles in *Clarissa*, I must observe how strictly the Author has kept up in all the Writings of his Rakes to what he says of *Lovelace* in his Preface.

'That they preserve a Decency, as well in their Images, as in their Language, which is not always to be found in the Works of some of the most celebrated modern Writers, whose Subjects and Characters have less warranted the Liberties they have taken.'

The various Stiles adapted to the many different [41] Characters in *Clarissa* make so great a Variety, as would, it attended to, in a great Measure, answer any Objection that might otherwise fairly be raised to the Length of the Story.

There is one Thing has almost astonished me in the Criticisms I have heard on *Clarissa's* Character; namely, that they are in a Manner a Counterpart to the Reproaches cast on her in her Lifetime.

She has been called perverse and obstinate by many of her Readers; *James Harlowe* called her so before them. Some say she was romantic; so said *Bella*; disobedient; all the *Harlowes* agree in that; a

Prude; so said *Salley Martin*; had a Mind incapable of Love; Mr. *Lovelace's* Accusation; for he must found his Brutality on some Shadow of a Pretence, tho' he confesses at last it was but a Shadow, for that he knew the contrary the whole Time. Others say, she was artful and cunning, had the Talent only to move the Passions; the haughty Brother and spiteful Sister's Plea to banish her from her Parents Presence. I verily think I have not heard *Clarissa* condemned for any one Fault, but the Author has made some of the *Harlowes*, or some of Mrs. *Sinclair's* Family accuse her of it before.

As I have, as concisely as I could, pointed out the Difference in the chief Characters of *Clarissa*, all necessary to the same End; in the same Manner could I go through the Scenes all as essentially different, and rising in due Proportion one after another, till all the vast Building centers in the pointed View of the Author's grand Design. Of all the lively well-painted Scenes in the four first Volumes, and all those in the fifth previous to the Night before the Outrage, mention but any of the most trifling Circumstances, such as *Clarissa's* torn Rufles, and Remembrance places her before us in all the [42] Agonies of the strongest Distress; insulted over by the vilest of Women, and prostrate on her Knees imploring Mercy at the Feet of her Destroyer. Her Madness equals, (I had almost said exceeds) any Thing of the Kind that ever was written: That hitherto so peculiar Beauty in King *Lear*, of preserving the Character even in Madness, appears strongly in *Clarissa*: the same self-accusing Spirit, the same humble Heart, the same pious Mind breathes in her scattered Scrapes of Paper in the midst of her Frenzy; and the Irregularity and sudden broken Starts of her Expressions alone can prove that her Senses are disordered. Her Letter to *Lovelace*, where, even in Madness, *galling* Reproach drops not from her Pen, and which contains only Supplications that she may not be farther persecuted, speaks the very Soul of *Clarissa*, and by the Author of her Story could have been wrote for no one but herself. Whoever can read her earnest Request to *Lovelace*, that she may not be exposed in a public Madhouse, on the Consideration that it might injure *him*, without being overwhelmed in Tears, I am certain has not in himself the Concord of sweet Sounds, and, must, as *Shakespear* says, be fit for Treasons, Stratagems and Spoils. And to close at once, all I will say of the Author's Conduct in regard to the managing (what seems most unmanageable) the Mind even when overcome by Madness, he has no where made a stronger Contrast between *Clarissa* and *Lovelace*, or kept the Characters more distinct than in their Madness. I have already mentioned how much *Clarissa's* Thoughts in her Frenzy apparently flow from the same Channel, tho' more disturbed and less clear than when her uninterrupted Reason kept on its steady Course. *Lovelace's* Character is not less preserved: his Pen or Tongue indeed seldom uttered the Words of Reason, but the same overbearing Passions, the same [43] Pride of Heart that had accustomed him to strut in his fancy'd Superiority, makes him condemn all the World but himself; and rave that *Bedlam* might be enlarged, imagining, that a general Madness had seized Mankind, and he alone was exempt from the dreadful Catastrophy.

In the Penknife Scene *Clarissa* is firmly brave; her Soul abhorred Self-murder, nor would she, as she told Miss *Howe*, willingly like a Coward quit her Post; but in this Case, could she not have awed *Lovelace* into Distance, tho' *her* Hand had pointed the Knife, yet might *he* properly have been said to have struck the Blow. The picturesque Attitude of all present, when *Clarissa* suddenly cries out, 'God's Eye is upon us' has an Effect upon the Mind that can only be felt; and that it would be a weak and vain Effort for Language to attempt to utter.

In the Prison Scene *Clarissa* exerts a different kind of Bravery. Insult and Distress, Cold and Hardships, to what she was accustomed to, she bears almost in silence; and by her Suffering without repining, without Fear of any thing but *Lovelace*, she is the strongest Proof of what *Shakespear* says, that

> *— —where the greater Malady is fixt*
> *The Lesser is scarce felt — —*

And let those who have accused *Clarissa* of having a suspicious Temper, from her being apt to suspect *Lovelace*, here confess, that it must be the Person's Fault at whom her Suspicion is level'd, when she wants that Companion of a great Mind, a generous Confidence; for how soon does *Belford's* honest Intentions breaking forth in the

Manner in which he addresses her, make her rely on the known Friend of her Destroyer, and the publick Companion of all his Rakeries. Nor can I here pass by in perfect Si [44] lence, the noble Simplicity with which *Clarissa* sums up her Story to Mrs. *Smith* and Mrs. *Lovick*; for I think 'tis the strongest Pattern that can be imagined of that Simplicity which strikes to the Heart, and melts the Soul with all the softer Passions.

In Colonel *Morden's* Account of the conveying the lifeless Remains of the Divine *Clarissa* to be interred in the Vault of her Ancestors, his very Words keep solemn Pace with the Herse which incloses her once animated, now lifeless, Form. Step by Step we still attend her; turn with the Horses as they take the Bye-road to *Harlow-place*; start with the wretched, guilty Family, at the first Stroke of the mournful tolling Bell; are fixed in Amazement with the lumbering heavy Noise of the Herse up the paved inner Court-yard: But when the Servant comes in to acquaint the Family with its Arrival, and we read this Line, *He spoke not, he could not speak; he looked, he bowed, and withdrew,* we catch the Servant's silent Grief; our Words are choaked, and our Sensations grow too strong for Utterance. The awful Respect paid to *Clarissa's* Memory by those Persons, who generally both rejoice and mourn in Noise and Clamour, is inimitably beautiful. But even in this solemn Scene the Author has not forgot the Characters of the principal Actors in it: For the barbarous Wretches who could drive *Clarissa* from her native Home, and by their Cruelty hurl her to Destruction, could not shed Tears for her Loss, without mingled Bitterness, and sharp-cutting Recriminations on each other; every one striving to rid themselves of the painful Load, and to throw it doubly on their former Companions in Guilt. The Mother only, as she was the least guilty, deplores the heavy Loss with soft melting Tears, and lets Self-accusations flow from her trembling Lips. [45]

On the Arrival of Miss *Howe*, we turn from the slow moving Herse, to the rapid Chariot-wheels that fly to bring the warm Friend, all glowing with the most poignant lively Grief, to mourn her lost *Clarissa*. Here again the Description equals the noble Subject. Miss *Howe*, at the first striking Sight of *Clarissa* in her Coffin, could only by frantic Actions express the labouring Anguish that perturbed her Breast. And we accompany her in Horror, when she first impatiently pushes aside the Coffin Lid. In short, we sigh, we rave, and we weep with her.

What I felt at Colonel *Morden's* Description at the Funeral, is exactly painted in the Letter wrote by Mr. *Belford* in Answer to that Description, where he says,

'You croud me Sir, methinks, into the silent, slow Procession — Now with the sacred Bier do I enter the Porch — ' [C]

But it would be endless to mention all the moving tragic Scenes, that are now crouding into my Mind, in *Clarissa*; all judiciously interspersed with Scenes of comic Humour; such as the Behaviour of *Lovelace* at the Ball; the Meeting between him and Mr. *Hickman*; *Lovelace's* Description of what he calls his Tryal before Lord M — and the Ladies; with some others equally calculated to relieve the Mind from fixing too long on mournful melancholy Ideas.

Finely has the Author of *Clarissa* set forth what is true, and what is false Honour. When *Lovelace* upbraids *Belford* for not preserving *Clarissa*, by betraying his own villainous Plots and Machinations to destroy her; and says, 'I am sure now, that I would have thanked thee for it with all my Heart, and thought thee more a Father and a Friend, than my real Father and my best Friend.'

[46]

All false Shame has he exposed, by shewing the Beauties of an open and frank Heart in *Clarissa's* charming Simplicity, when she tells Mrs. *Smith*, in a publick Shop, that she had been in Prison; and when in a Letter to Lady *Betty Laurance* she declares, that *the Disgrace she cannot hide from herself, she is not sollicitous to conceal from the World.*

True and false Friendship was never more beautifully displayed than in this Work; the firm, the steady Flame that burns in the fixed Affection between *Clarissa* and Miss *Howe*, which, in *Clarissa's* Words, *has Virtue for its Base*, is both well described and accounted for by Colonel *Morden*; and that Chaff and Stubble, as she well calls it, that *has not Virtue for its Base*, is inimitably painted by *Belford*, in his Account of *Mowbray's* Behaviour to the dying *Belton*. 'It is such a horrid thing (says he) to think of, that a Man who had lived in such strict Terms of Amity with another (the Proof does not come out so as to say Friendship) who had pretended so much Love for him, could not bear to be out of his Company, would ride an hundred Miles an End to enjoy it, and would fight for him, be the Cause right or wrong; yet now could be so little moved to see him in such Misery of Body and Mind as to be able to rebuke him, and rather ridicule than pity him; because he was more affected by what he felt, than he had seen a Malefactor (hardened perhaps by Liquor, and not softened by previous Sickness) on his going to Execution.'

What Merit has *Clarissa* in breaking up and dispersing this profligate Knot of Friends, that, in the first Volume, are represented so formidable as to terrify all the honest People in the Neighbourhood, who rejoice when they go up to Town again. *She* was to revenge on *Lovelace* his Miss *Betterton*, his *French* Devotee, his *French* Countess, the whole [47] Hecatomb which he boasts that he had in different Climes sacrificed to his *Nemesis*, and all this by the natural Effects of his own vile Actions, and her honest noble Simplicity; whilst she steadily pursues the bright Path of Innocence, and proposes to herself no other End, no not even in Thought, but to preserve untainted her spotless Mind, and diffuse Happiness to all around her.

I confess I was against the Story's ending unhappily, till I saw the Conclusion; but I now think the different Deaths of the many Persons (for in this Point also the Difference is as essentially preserved, as in the Characters or Scenes) who fall in the winding up the Catastrophy in the seventh Volume, produce as noble a Moral as can be invented by the Wit of Man.

The broken Spirit, the dejected Heart that pursue poor *Belton* through his last Stage of Life (brought on by a lingering Illness, and ill Usage from an artful Woman to whom Vice had attached him, and increased by his Soul's being startled and awaked from that thoughtless Lethargy in which Vice had so long lulled him) naturally break forth in those fearful Tremors, those agonizing pannic Terrors of the Mind, which follow him to the End, and make a strong and lively Picture of the Terrors of Death first thought on, when Life was flying, and could no longer supply the flowing Blood and vital Heat that animates the mortal Frame.

Mrs. *Sinclair's* Death is very different; the Suddenness of her Departure had not given Time for a regular Decay of her Strength, and the same animal Spirits which used to support her in the noisy Roar of a profligate Life, now like so many Vultures preyed on her own Bosom, and assisted to express the dreadful Horrors of an unexpected Death. [48]

Lovelace, when he comes to die, is full of Rage and Disappointment; his uncontrouled Spirit, unused to be baffled, cannot quietly submit to the great and universal Conqueror Death himself. On his Death-bed he is a lively Picture of the End of that worldly Wisdom which is Foolishness with God. His strong Imagination that assisted him to form and carry on those *cunning* Plots which he pursued to his own Destruction, now assisted his Conscience to torment his Soul, and set before his Eyes the injured Innocent who would have contributed to the utmost of her Power that he might have spent all his Days in Peace and Joy. In short, he fluttered like a gay Butterfly in the Sunshine of Prosperity; he wandered from the Path that leads to Happiness: In the Bloom of Youth he fell a Sacrifice to his own Folly: his Life was a Life of Violence, and his Death was a Death of Rage.

Whilst the gentle *Clarissa's* Death is the natural Consequence of her innocent Life; her calm and prepared Spirit, like a soft smooth Stream, flows gently on, till it slides from her Misfortunes, and she leaves the World free from Fear, and animated only by a lively Hope.

She wished her closing Scene might be happy. *She had her Wish,* (says the Author in his Postscript) *it was happy.*

Nothing ever made so strong a Contrast as the Deaths of *Lovelace* and *Clarissa*. Wild was the Life of *Lovelace*, rapid was his Death; gentle was *Clarissa's* Life, softly flowed her latest Hours; the very Word *Death* seems too harsh to describe her leaving Life, and her last Breath was like the soft playing of a western Breeze, all calm! all Peace! all Quiet! [49]

The true Difference between the Virtuous and the Vicious lies in the Mind, where the Author of *Clarissa* has placed it; *Lovelace* says well, when he views the persecuted *Clarissa* a-sleep.

'See the Difference in our Cases; she the charming Injured can sweetly sleep, whilst the varlet Injurer cannot close his Eyes, and has been trying to no purpose the whole Night to divert his Melancholy, and to fly from himself.'

Rightly I think in the Author's Postscript is it observed, that what is called poetical Justice is chimerical, or rather anti-providential Justice; for God makes his Sun to shine alike on the Just and the Unjust. Why then should Man invent a kind of imaginary Justice, making the common Accidents of Life turn out favourable to the Virtuous only? Vain would be the Comforts spoken to the Virtuous in Affliction, in the sacred Writings, if Affliction could not be their Lot.

But the Author of *Clarissa* has in his Postscript quoted such undoubted Authorities, and given so many Reasons on the Christian System for his Catastrophy, that to say more on that Head would be but repeating his Words. The Variety of Punishments also of those guilty Persons in this Work who do not die, and the Rewards of those who are innocent, I could go through; had not that Postscript, and the Conclusion supposed to be writ by Mr. *Belford,* already done it to my Hands. Only one thing I must say, that I don't believe the most revengeful Person upon Earth could wish their worst Enemy in a more deplorable Situation, than if *Lovelace* in his Frenzy, in that charming picturesque Scene, where he is riding between *Uxbridge* and *London,* when his impatient Spirit is in suspence; and also when he hears of *Clarissa's* Death. [50]

Thus have I just hinted at the Heads of the Characters, the Difference of the chief Scenes, and the Variety of the several Deaths, all the natural Consequences of the several Lives, and productive of the designed noble Moral in *Clarissa;* and I think it may be fairly and impartially said, The Web is wove so strongly, every Part so much depending on and assisting each other, that to divide any of them, would be to destroy the whole.

> [D] *That many Things having full References*
> *To one Consent, may work contrariously:*
> *As many Arrows, loosed several Ways,*
> *Come to one Mark, as many Ways meet in one Town,*
> *As many fresh Streams meet in one salt Sea,*
> *As many Lines close in the Dial's Center,*
> *So may a thousand Actions once afoot*

End in one Purpose, and be all well born
Without Defeat.

43

If what I have here said can be any Amusement to you, as it concerns your favourite *Clarissa*, my End will be answered. I am,

Miss GIBSON *to* BELLARIO.

SIR ,

Y OUR Good-nature in sending me your Thoughts on *Clarissa,* with a Design to give me Pleasure, I assure you is not thrown away; may [51] you have equal Success in every generous Purpose that fills your Heart, and greater Happiness in this World, I am sure I cannot wish you.

Most truly, Sir, do you remark, that a Story told in this Manner can move but slowly, that the Characters can be seen only by such as attend strictly to the Whole; yet this Advantage the Author gains by writing in the present Tense, as he himself calls it, and in the first Person, that his Strokes penetrate immediately to the Heart, and we feel all the Distresses he paints; we not only weep for, but with *Clarissa,* and accompany her, step by step, through all her Distresses.

I see her from the Beginning, in her happy State, beloved by all around her, studying to deserve that Love; obedient to her Parents, dependant on their Will by her own voluntary Act, when her Grandfather had put it in her Power to be otherwise; respectful and tender to her Brother and Sister; firm in her Friendship to Miss *Howe;* grateful to good Mrs. *Norton,* who had carefully watched over her Infant Years, and delighted to form and instruct her Mind; kind to her Inferiors; beneficent to all the Poor, Miserable, and Indigent; and above all, cultivating and cherishing in her Heart the true Spirit of Christianity, Meekness, and Resignation; watchful over her own Conduct, and charitable to the Failings of others; unwilling to condemn, and rejoicing in every Opportunity to praise. But as the Laws of God and Man have placed a Woman totally in the Power of her Husband, I believe it is utterly impossible for any young Woman, who has any Reflection, not to form in her Mind some kind of Picture of the Sort of Man in whose Power she would chuse to place herself. That *Clarissa* did so, I think, plainly appears, from her steady Resolution [52] to refuse any Man she could not obey with the utmost Chearfulness; and to whose Will she could not submit without Reluctance. She would have had her Husband a Man on whose Principles she could entirely depend; one in whom she might have placed such a Confidence, that she might have spoke her very Thoughts aloud; one from whom she might have gained Instruction, and from whose Superiority of Understanding she would have been pleased to have taken the Rules of her own Actions. She desired no Reserves, no separate Interest from her Husband; had no Plots, no Machinations to succeed in, and therefore wanted not a Man who by artful Flattery she could have cajoled madly to have worship'd her; a kind Indulgence, in what was reasonable, was all her Desire, and that Indulgence to arise from her own Endeavour to deserve it, and not from any Blindness cast before her Husband's Eyes by dazzling Beauty, or cunning Dissimulation; but, from her Infancy, having the Example daily before her of her Mother's being tyrannized over, notwithstanding her great Humility and Meekness, perhaps tyrannized over for that very Humility and Meekness. She thought a single Life, in all Probability, would be for her the happiest; cherishing in her Heart that Characteristic of a noble Mind, especially in a Woman, of wishing, as Miss *Howe* says she did, to pass through Life unnoted.

In this State of Mind did *Lovelace* first find *Clarissa*. She liked him; his Person and Conversation were agreeable, but the Libertinism of his Character terrified her; and her Disapprobation of him restrained her from throwing the Reins over the Neck of a Passion she thought might have hurried her into Ruin. But when by his Artifices, and the Cruelty of her Friends, she was driven into his Power, had [53] he not, to use her own Words, treated her with an Insolence unbecoming a Man, and kept her very Soul in suspence; fawning at her Feet to marry him, whilst, in the same Instant, he tried to confuse her by a Behaviour that put it out of her Power to comply with him; there was nothing that she would not have done to oblige him. Then indeed she plainly saw that her Principles and his Profligacy, her Simplicity and his Cunning, were not made to be joined; and when she found such was the Man she liked best, no Wonder her Desire of a single Life should return. She saw, indeed, her own Superiority over *Lovelace*, but it was his Baseness that made her behold it. And here I must observe, that in the very same Breath in which she tells him, *Her Soul's above him*, she bids him *leave her*, that Thought more than any other makes her resolve, at all Events, to abandon him. Was this like exulting in her own Understanding, and proudly (as I have heard it said) wanting to dictate to the Man she intended for a Husband? Such a Woman, if I am not greatly mistaken, would not desire the Man to leave her because she saw her Soul was above him; but on the contrary, concealing from him, and disguising her Thoughts, would have set Art against Art, and been the more delighted to have drawn him in to have married her, that she might have deceived him, and enjoyed the Thoughts of her own Superiority for Life. As I remember, he never asks her fairly to marry him but once, and then she consents: But how different in every Action is she from the sly and artful Woman, who would have snatched at this Opportunity, and not have trusted him with a Moment's Delay, whilst *Clarissa*, being then ill, consents, with a Confidence that nothing but her Goodness and Simplicity could have had in such a Man. [54]

Tho' *Clarissa* unfortunately met with *Lovelace*, yet I can imagine her with a Lover whose honest Heart, assimulating with hers, would have given her leave, as she herself wishes, to have shewn the Frankness of her Disposition, and to have openly avowed her Love. But *Lovelace*, by his own intriguing Spirit, made her Reserves, and then complained of them; and as she was engaged with such a Man, I think the Catastrophe's being what is called *Unhappy*, is but the natural Consequence of such an Engagement; tho', I confess, I was not displeased that the Report of this Catastrophe met with so many Objections, as it proved what an Impression the Author's favourite Character had made on those Minds which could not bear she should fall a Sacrifice to the Barbarity of her Persecutors. And I hope that now all the Readers of *Clarissa* are convinced how rightly the Author has judged in this Point. If the Story was not to have ended tragically, the grand Moral would have been lost, as well as that grand Picture, if I may call it so, of human Life, of a Man's giving up every thing that is valuable, only because every thing that is valuable is in his Power. *Lovelace* thought of the Substance, whilst that was yet to be persued; but once within reach of it, his plotting Head and roving Imagination would let him see only the Shadow, and once enter'd into the Pursuit, his Pride, the predominant Passion of his Soul, engaged him to fly after a visionary Gratification which his own wild Fancy had painted, till, like one following an *Ignis fatuus* through By-Paths and crooked Roads, he lost himself in

the Eagerness of his own Pursuit, and involved with him the innocent *Clarissa*, who, persecuted, misunderstood, envied, and evil-
treated as she had been, by those from whom she had most Reason
to hope Protection, I think could not find a better Close to her [55]
Misfortunes than a triumphant Death. Triumphant it may very well
be called, when her Soul, fortified by a truly Christian Philosophy,
melted and softened in the School of Affliction, had conquered every earthly Desire, baffled every uneasy Passion, lost every disturb-
ing Fear, while nothing remained in her tender Bosom but a lively
Hope of future Happiness. When her very Griefs were in a manner
forgot, the Impression of them as faint and languid as a feverish
Dream to one restored to Health, all calm and serene her Mind,
forgiving and praying for her worst Enemies, she retired from all
her Afflictions, to meet the Reward of her Christian Piety.

The Death of *Clarissa* is, I believe, the only Death of the Kind in
any Story; and in her Character, the Author has thrown into Action
(if I may be allowed the Expression) the true Christian Philosophy,
shewn its Force to ennoble the human Mind, till it can look with
Serenity on all human Misfortunes, and take from Death itself its
gloomy Horrors. Never was any thing more judicious than the Author's bringing *Lovelace* as near as *Knight's-Bridge* at the Time of
Clarissa's Death; for by that means he has in a manner contrived to
place in one View before our Eyes the guilty Ravager of unprotected
Innocence, the boasting Vaunter of his own useless Parts, in all the
Horrors of mad Despair, whilst the injured Innocent, in a pious, in a
divine Frame of Mind is peaceably breathing her last. 'Such a Smile!
such a charming Serenity (says Mr. *Belford*) overspreading her sweet
Face at the Instant, as seemed to manifest her eternal Happiness
already begun.'

Surely the Tears we shed for *Clarissa* in her last Hours, must be
Tears of tender Joy! Whilst we [56] seem to live, and daily converse
with her through her last Stage, our Hearts are at once rejoiced and
amended, are both soften'd and elevated, till our Sensations grow
too strong for any Vent, but that of Tears; nor am I ashamed to confess, that Tears without Number have I shed, whilst Mr. *Belford* by
his Relation has kept me (as I may say) with fixed Attention in her
Apartment, and made me perfectly present at her noble exalted
Behaviour; nor can I hardly refrain from crying out, 'Farewell, my

dear *Clarissa*! may every Friend I love in this World imitate you in their Lives, and thus joyfully quit all the Cares and Troubles that disturb this mortal Being!'

May *Clarissa's* Memory be as triumphant as was her Death! May all the World, like *Lovelace*, bear Testimony to her Virtues, and acknowledge her Triumph!

I am with many Thanks, Sir, for your obliging Letter,

> *Yo*
> *ur*
> *most*
> *obe-*
> *dient,*
> &c.

These Letters were shewn me by Miss *Gibson*, and thus, Sir, have I collected together all I have heard on your History of *Clarissa*; and if every thing that Miss *Gibson* and *Bellario* has said, is fairly deducible from the Story, then I am certain, by the candid and good-natured Reader, this will be deemed a fair and impartial Examination, tho' I avow myself the sincere Admirer of *Clarissa*, and

Your very humble Servant,

F I N I S .

FOOTNOTES

[A] *Pope's Homer.*

[B] Othello.

[C] See Vol. VII. Letter 74. Page 292. in *Clarissa*.

[D] See *Shakespear's Henry* the Vth.